How to Read to a Grandma or Grandpa

By **Jean Reagan**

Illustrated by **Lee Wildish**

ALFRED A. KNOPF

NEW YORK

For all readers, especially the brand-new readers —J.R.

To all grandmas and grandpas —L.W.

THIS IS A BORZOI BOOK PUBLISHED BY ALFRED A. KNOPF

Text copyright © 2020 by Jean Reagan
Jacket art and interior illustrations copyright © 2020 by Lee Wildish

Visit us on the Web! rhcbooks.com

Educators and librarians, for a variety of teaching tools, visit us at RHTeachersLibrarians.com

Library of Congress Cataloging-in-Publication Data is available upon request.
ISBN 978-1-5247-0193-2 (trade) — ISBN 978-1-5247-0194-9 (lib. bdg.) — ISBN 978-1-5247-0195-6 (ebook)

The text of this book is set in 18-point Gotham Book.
The illustrations were created digitally.
Book design by Jinna Shin

MANUFACTURED IN CHINA
July 2020
10 9 8 7 6 5 4 3 2 1
First Edition

Reading is a blast! But if you want to make it
extra fun, read to a grandma or grandpa!

First, help them pick a book.

WHERE TO FIND A GOOD BOOK:

- **On the bookshelf**

In your bed

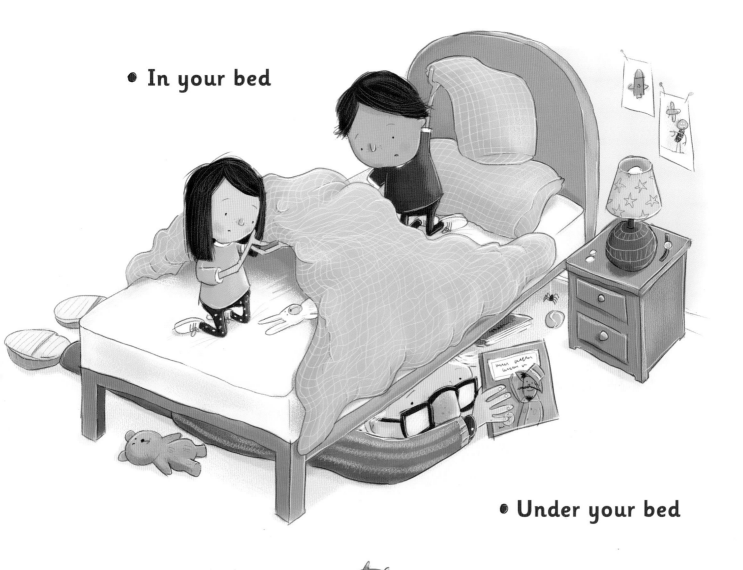

Under your bed

In the car

Then ask,

"WHAT ARE YOUR FAVORITE THINGS TO READ ABOUT?"

Did you find a great book? If not, take your grandma to choose a new one.

OTHER PLACES TO LOOK FOR BOOKS:

- **A bookstore**

The library

Your classroom

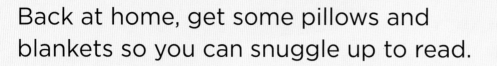

Back at home, get some pillows and blankets so you can snuggle up to read.

For grandparents who live far away, show them how to snuggle up, long-distance.

Now you're ready to start.

(Oops. Not yet—where
are those reading glasses?)

Okay, NOW you're ready.

Next, show them different
ways to turn the page.

HOW TO TURN THE PAGE:

- **A super-funny page: turn back to it—
  again and again—until your grandma
  is all worn out from laughing.**

- **A scary page:** offer to peek ahead to make sure things don't get *too* spooky.

- **A fragile page from Grandpa's old book:** turn it slowly and softly.

When you finish the book,
decide together how much
you liked it.

Then ask your grandma, "What was *your* favorite part?" See if she can guess yours.

After reading a stack of books, your grandpa or grandma may get antsy. That means—time to get up and play!

HOW TO PLAY TOGETHER:

- **Act out the book: stretch and stomp like a ninja-dinosaur.**

- Try a science experiment from your book. Or a recipe.

- Build something tall so you can "Crash! Bang! Kaboom!"

If you ever want to make their storytime *extra* special, read to your grandpa or grandma in a brand-new place:

• **Bug books in a garden**

CHECKLIST for BUGS

THE GUIDE TO TRUCKS

TRUCKS LIST

• **Truck books near a construction site**

• Ballet books while you wait
  for a performance to begin

• Snowy-day books on a sled

Or . . . an owl book by the light of a full moon.

But no matter *where* you read
or *what* you read . . .

. . . when you get to "The End," your grandma or grandpa will probably ask, "Can you read to me again, please?" Of course, you'll say—

"YES!"